Hello, Family Members,

Learning to read is one of the most important accomplishments of early childhood. **Hello Reader!** books are designed to help children become skilled readers who like to read. Beginning readers learn to read by remembering frequently used words like "the," "is," and "and"; by using phonics skills to decode new words; and by interpreting picture and text clues. These books provide both the stories children enjoy and the structure they need to read fluently and independently. Here are suggestions for helping your child *before*, *during*, and *after* reading:

Before

- Look at the cover and pictures and have your child predict what the story is about.
- Read the story to your child.
- Encourage your child to chime in with familiar words and phrases.
- Echo read with your child by reading a line first and having your child read it after you do.

During

- Have your child think about a word he or she does not recognize right away. Provide hints such as "Let's see if we know the sounds" and "Have we read other words like this one?"
- Encourage your child to use phonics skills to sound out new words.
- Provide the word for your child when more assistance is needed so that he or she does not struggle and the experience of reading with you is a positive one.
- Encourage your child to have fun by reading with a lot of expression . . . like an actor!

After

- Have your child keep lists of interesting and favorite words.
- Encourage your child to read the books over and over again. Have him or her read to brothers, sisters, grandparents, and even teddy bears. Repeated readings develop confidence in young readers.
- Talk about the stories. Ask and answer questions. Share ideas about the funniest and most interesting characters and events in the stories.

I do hope that you and your child enjoy this book.

—Francie Alexander
Reading Specialist,
Scholastic's Instructional Publishing Group

If you have questions or comments about how children learn to read, please contact Francie Alexander at FrancieAl@aol.com

NEW LINE CINEMA PRESENTS A PRELUDE PICTURES PRODUCTION IN ASSOCIATION WITH IRWIN ALLEN PRODUCTIONS A STEPHEN HOPKINS FILM GARY OLDMAN WILLIAM HURT 'LOST IN SPACE' MATT LeBLANC MIMI ROGERS HEATHER GRAHAM JARED HARRIS LACEY CHABERT JACK JOHNSON ANIMATRONIC CREATURES BY JIM HENSON'S CREATURE SHOP FILM EDITOR RAY LOVEJOY

SDDS Sony Cinema Digital Sound PRODUCTION DESIGNED BY NORMAN GARWOOD DIRECTOR OF PHOTOGRAPHY PETER LEVY, A.C.S. CO-EXECUTIVE PRODUCER MICHAEL ILITCH, JR. EXECUTIVE PRODUCERS MACE NEUFELD BOB REHME RICHARD SAPERSTEIN MICHAEL DE LUCA DOLBY DIGITAL

THIS FILM NOT YET RATED PRODUCED BY MARK W. KOCH STEPHEN HOPKINS AKIVA GOLDSMAN CARLA FRY WRITTEN BY AKIVA GOLDSMAN DIRECTED BY STEPHEN HOPKINS NEW LINE CINEMA © 1998 NEW LINE PRODUCTIONS, INC. ALL RIGHTS RESERVED

Photos by Jack English and Milly Donaghy

ISBN 0-590-18937-9

10   9   8   7   6   5   4   3   2   8   9/9   0/0   01   02

Book design by Alfred Giuliani
Printed in the U.S.A.   23
First Scholastic printing, April 1998

LOST IN SPACE ™

Adapted by Gina Shaw

Based on the screenplay
written by Akiva Goldsman

Hello Reader!—Level 4

SCHOLASTIC INC.

Cartwheel BOOKS ®

New York   Toronto   London   Auckland   Sydney

✧ INTRODUCTION ✧

Earth was very sick.
Food and water were running out.
The people had to go to a different planet
called Alpha Prime in order to live.
Ten-year-old Will Robinson and his family
were to be the first to go to this new
world.
A pilot, Major Don West, would fly their
spaceship, the *Jupiter 2*.
Will and his family would have to fly
for ten years to reach Alpha Prime!
Once there, they would build a
"hypergate," a kind of doorway in space.
The hypergate would allow people
to travel from Earth to the new world
instantly!
But an evil man named Dr. Smith wanted
to stop the ship from reaching the planet.
He snuck on to the *Jupiter 2*.

There he programmed a robot
to blow up the ship.
But the doctor was unable to leave
before the ship took off.
Now, Dr. Smith, Major West, and the
Robinson family are racing through space.
And the robot is about to follow
the doctor's orders.
Can this mission—and the people
of planet Earth—be saved?

✧ CHAPTER 1 ✧

***Setting: A lower deck on the* Jupiter 2**

All was quiet on the *Jupiter 2*.
Major Don West and the Robinson family
were sleeping in special tubes.
The tubes were supposed to keep them

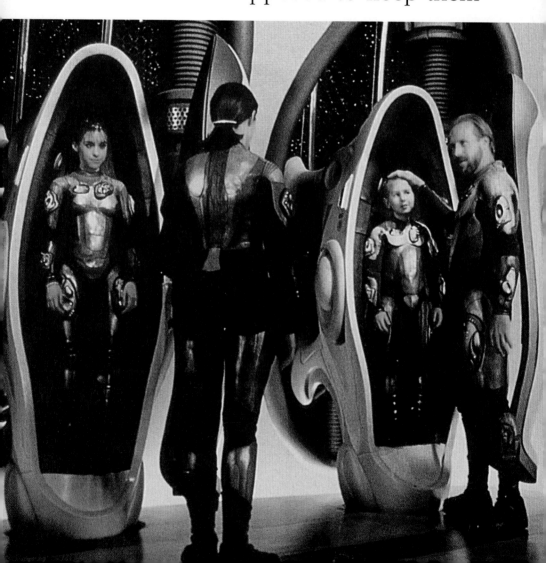

asleep for the entire ten-year trip.

But a loud voice broke the silence.

"Robinson family, destroy!"

It was the robot that had been programmed by Dr. Smith.

The frightened doctor was the only person awake on the ship.

He looked up to see the giant robot coming toward him.

Robot extended its arms and fired.

The shots hit the control panel and knocked the ship off course.

Will Robinson and his sister Penny awoke to find their ship rocking and shaking.

Their parents, Professor John Robinson and his wife Maureen, ran to Major West at the controls.

The *Jupiter 2* was heading straight for the sun!

John tried to stop Robot while Major West worked to gain control of the ship.

But John was no match for
Robot's strength.
Just when all hope seemed lost,
Robot suddenly stopped.
John looked over to see his son, Will,
holding his tiny computer in his hands.
"Robot," said Will. "Go to your
docking bay."
"Command accepted," said Robot.
Will smiled. "If the family won't come
to the science fair," he said, "bring the
science fair to the family!"
John looked at his son in amazement.
Back on Earth, Will had accused
his father of ignoring him.
John knew Will was right.
All of John's attention had been
taken up by this mission.
He had even missed his own
son's science fair.
Will had won first place for his model
of a time machine.

Now the boy had used his "hacker deck," a tiny computer, to stop Robot. John promised himself that when they got to Alpha Prime, he would spend more time with Will.

From the control panel, Major West
glared at Dr. Smith.
"You caused this trouble,"
Major West said.
He realized that Dr. Smith wasn't
even supposed to be on the ship.
But there was no time to argue
with the doctor.

The ship was shaking in the
mighty pull of the sun.
"There's got to be some way to get
through this," John said.
"There is!" Major West answered. "If
we can't go around the sun, we have
to go through it. We'll use the
hyperdrive."
The crew knew that the hyperdrive
was dangerous.
It would send them anywhere
in the galaxy.
Without a hypergate or doorway,
there was no way to control where
they would wind up.
Still, it was their only hope.
Major West put the *Jupiter 2*
into hyperdrive.
The ship hurled toward the sun.
Then it disappeared into hyperspace.
In a flash, the *Jupiter 2* reappeared.
But where were they?

✧ CHAPTER 2 ✧

Setting: Lost in space

Major West and John looked into
the deep, dark space around them.
They saw something that looked
like a hole.
Through it, they could see a giant
silver ship.
Maybe the ship could help them find
out where they were.
Major West took their ship through
the hole in space.
Then he attached the *Jupiter 2* to the
giant ship.
He joined John, Will's sister Judy,
and Robot as they boarded the ship
and began to explore.
John forced Dr. Smith to come, too.
He was afraid to leave the doctor
on the *Jupiter 2.*

Inside the strange ship, a room was
filled with plants and vines.
Major West moved some leaves and saw
an alien creature.
The creature looked like a small monkey
with bright blue eyes.

"No one's going to hurt you," said the major to the frightened creature. The creature held on tightly to Major West's neck.
"Looks like you've made a friend," said Judy.

They named their new companion Blawp
because of the funny *blawp* sounds
it made.
Together the group walked on.
They noticed that the ceiling was covered
with rows and rows of jagged holes.
Before their eyes, the holes began to shake.
Suddenly, a monster out of a nightmare
burst through the ceiling!

The creature had a shiny metal body
and spiderlike arms and legs.
All at once, many more spiders
dropped in behind the first one.
The crew of the *Jupiter 2* shot
at the spiders.

Then they raced down the long
hallway back to their ship.
But their shots had set off an alarm.

The door at the end of the hallway
slammed shut.

They were trapped!

The spiders swarmed closer and closer.

Then a loud crash echoed at the
end of the hallway.

Robot had blown a hole in the door.

Judy hurried through the hole
carrying Blawp.

John, Major West, and Dr. Smith followed.

The crew ran toward their ship as Robot moved in front of the hole to block the spiders.

The greedy creatures began to eat away at Robot's metal body.

The door to the *Jupiter 2* started to close just as the crew ran inside.

But not before one of the spiders scratched Dr. Smith!

Though inside their ship, the crew
was not out of danger.
The spiders attached themselves
to the *Jupiter 2.*
Thinking fast, Major West blew up
the other ship.
The blast destroyed the spiders.
But it also knocked the *Jupiter 2*
onto a giant planet below.

✧ CHAPTER 3 ✧

Setting: On the new planet

The spaceship landed with a crash
on the new planet.
Will sat at the main computer.
Though Robot's body had been destroyed
by the spiders, Will had saved its mind.
He had stored Robot's memory
in his hacker deck.
"Can you hear me?" asked Will. "Robot?"
The voice of Robot spoke from the
computer screen. "Robot tried to destroy
the Robinson family. Why did Will
Robinson save Robot?"
Will smiled. "I guess sometimes
friendship means listening to your heart,
not your head," he said. "I'm going to
build you a new body."

21

The *Jupiter 2* crew gathered together.
Their ship was damaged.
They needed materials to help them
get off the planet.
The computer told them that the planet
was filled with many doorways.
The doorways led into the future
and they were constantly opening
and closing.
They were tearing the planet apart.
John thought the doorways were
a natural part of the planet.
But Will had another idea.
"These doorways are exactly what
I said my time machine would do!"
Will said excitedly. "What if—"
"Son," John interrupted. "I appreciate
your help, but now isn't the time
to use your imagination."
"You never listen to me!" shouted Will.
"Not ever!"

Once again, John had hurt
his son's feelings.
But there was no time to apologize.
They had to search for materials
to fix their ship.
John and Major West left to begin
the search.
They stepped outside and walked
through a shining doorway.
Both men were whisked away
into the future.

✧ ✧ ✧ ✧ ✧

Setting: Back inside the Jupiter 2

Meanwhile, an upset Will returned
to work on Robot.
From down the hall, he heard
a knocking sound.
"It sounds like Morse code,"
said Robot.
"What is it saying?" Will asked.
"Danger, Will Robinson, danger!"
Robot answered.
Will followed the sound of the
knocking.
He found Dr. Smith in his room.
Dr. Smith had a secret plan.
He wanted to take control of the ship.
The doctor told Will that his father
was in great danger.
Will agreed to go with Dr. Smith.
They followed John and Major West
into the future.

✧ CHAPTER 4 ✧

Setting: On the planet, many years into the future

John and Major West walked through
many of the strange doorways.
They came upon a wrecked ship
at the edge of a crater wall.
The lower sections were gone.
The hull was scarred.
They realized that this was their ship,
the *Jupiter 2*, many years into the future.
Major West and John entered the ship.
A tall figure walked toward them.
It was a man who looked strangely
familiar to both of them.
"Who are you?" John asked.
The figure answered, "Don't you
recognize me, Dad? I'm your son, Will."

John and Major West stared at this
Older Will in shock.
Then they turned to see Robot
coming toward them.
Robot forced them to follow
Older Will inside a large room.
As a child, Older Will had rebuilt
Robot's body.
He had also spent the past twenty
years building something else.

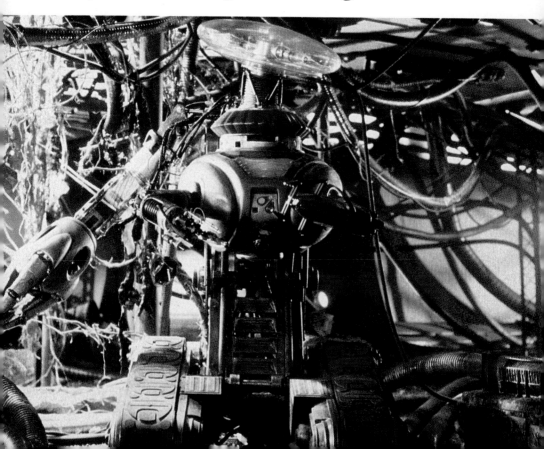

"Look what I've done," said Older Will. "I built my time machine!"
John and Major West saw that the time machine was using the material they needed to fix their ship.
Older Will planned to use his machine to open a doorway in time.
Only one person would be able to make the trip through time and space.
"I will be able to return home to the very day you took us on this mission," said Older Will. "I'll stop us from taking off. I'll save the family."
"Your machine is ripping this planet apart," John answered. "It could do the same to Earth. What if, in getting home, you destroy the Earth in the process?"
But Older Will refused to listen.
His father had never been there for him as a child.
Now Older Will would travel back to the past and change the future.

"I can save us all," said Older Will.
"I'm afraid not," said a voice.
The group turned to see Dr. Smith
pushing Young Will into the room.
As the doctor had planned, Young Will
had led him straight to John and
Major West.

But the situation was even better than
Dr. Smith had hoped.
With Older Will's time machine,
Dr. Smith could take the one trip
through time and escape from the planet.
He could return to Earth.

Dr. Smith's plan seemed perfect until
a strange but somehow familiar voice
echoed through the ship.
"Never fear, Smith is here!"
A frightening shape moved toward
Dr. Smith.
First its arms and then its legs unfolded.
It stood ten feet tall.
The creature was half-spider and
half-Dr. Smith!
Dr. Smith watched in horror.
He remembered the scratch
he had gotten earlier while racing
away from the spiders.
Now he saw himself in the future.
The scratch had caused him
to become half-man, half-spider.
This Future Smith threw Dr. Smith
out of the ship, then ordered Robot
to guard everyone.

Future Smith followed Older Will
to the top of the time machine.
The creature had an evil plan of his own.
He would take Older Will's place
and travel to Earth.
Once there, he would take over
the entire planet!

The group watched helplessly as
Future Smith and Older Will disappeared
up the ramp.
Robot stood guard.
Young Will walked over to his old friend.
"Robot, do you remember what I taught
you about friendship?" Young Will asked.

Robot answered, "Friendship means acting with your heart, not your head." "I need you to help us now," said Will. "We're friends. Act with your heart."
Suddenly, the ship shook again.
The planet was coming apart.
Will begged, "Please, Robot, will you help us?"
"Robot will save..." Robot answered. "I will save Will Robinson. I will save my friend!"

✧ CHAPTER 5 ✧

With Robot once again on their side,
the group left the ship.
But doorways were opening and
closing all around them.
Which one would lead them home?

Then they looked through one of the
doorways and saw a familiar sight.
Judy, Maureen, and Penny had used
lights from the *Jupiter 2* to form
a sign in the sky.
"Jump!" shouted Major West.
He, Dr. Smith, Young Will, and Robot
all passed through the doorway.

They found themselves back
on the *Jupiter 2* in their own time.
But one person did not follow.
John had stayed behind.
He knew their ship still needed
the material to escape the planet.
Slowly, he made his way up the ramp
where Future Smith was waiting.

John reached the top of the ramp.
He saw Future Smith walking toward
the doorway of the time machine.
The creature had thrown Older Will
out of the way, knocking him out.
Future Smith and John fought
with each other.
The creature tumbled backward
over a rail.
John watched as Future Smith was
washed away by the tides of time.
Then he saw Older Will hanging over the
rail where Future Smith had thrown him.
The time machine was about to use up
all of the material that John needed.
John had to make a quick decision—get
the material or save Older Will?
He grabbed Will's wrist at the
last second!
"I thought I lost you," John said
to his son.

"You could have taken the material and left before it was too late," Older Will said. "You saved me instead."

"There wasn't any choice," John answered. "I couldn't let you fall. You're my boy."

Just then, Older Will changed the setting
on the time machine.
Instead of a doorway back to Earth,
the machine now led back to the
Jupiter 2 in John's time.

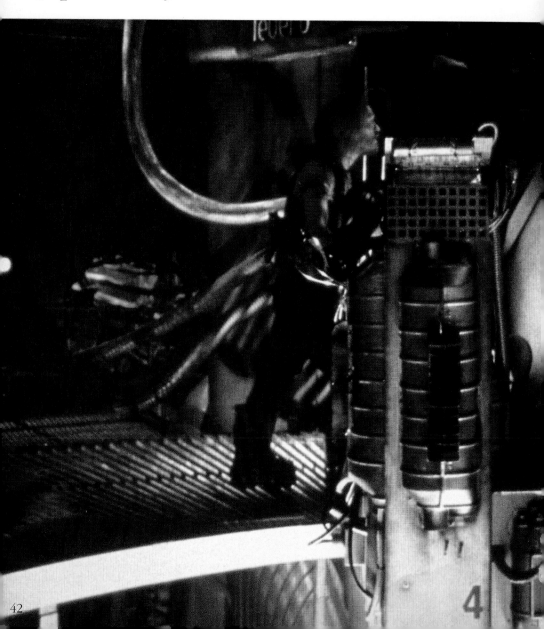

Older Will looked at his father.
He knew he had the power to send
John back to his family — back to
Young Will who needed him.

"Don't make me wait another lifetime
to know how you feel," Older Will said.
"Come with us," said John.
But Older Will couldn't come.
Only one person could make the trip.
John passed through the doorway and
landed back on the *Jupiter 2.*

As the doorway closed on Older Will forever, John held Young Will tightly. "I just want you to know," John said to his son, "I love you very much."

Setting: Back on the Jupiter 2 in the present

Jupiter 2's crew (and Blawp, too!) were all together again. Robot had even found their

location on a star map.
They were not lost anymore.
But their ship was in trouble.
"The planet is breaking up around
us," said Major West.
"There's no way to get clear in time,"
John added.

"The hyperdrive," Judy suggested.
The crew knew the hyperdrive
could be used without the material
John had left behind.
But where would it send them?
Maureen said, "Everyone hang on!"
"Here we go again," said Penny.
"Cool!" said Will.
Major West threw the switch.
The planet exploded as the *Jupiter 2*
vanished into hyperspace.
It was far away from Earth and
far away from Alpha Prime.
Once again, the *Jupiter 2* was
lost in space.

The End?